MW01064738

The Slumber Girls and The Mystical Dollhouse

The Slumber Girls and The Mystical Dollhouse

By Ann Carpenter

Ann Carpenter

Kidz by Dezign Press
Lawrenceville, GA
United States of America

PUBLISHED BY

Kidz By Dezign Press, 1881 Kingston Way
Lawrenceville, GA 30044

Kidz By Dezign Press, 1881 Kingston Way
Lawrenceville, GA 30044

Publisher's Cataloging-In-Publication Data
(Prepared by The Donohue Group, Inc.)

Carpenter, Ann, 1939-
The Slumber Girls and the mystical dollhouse / by Ann Carpenter.

p. ; cm.
Includes bibliographical references.
ISBN: 0-9771030-0-5

1. Queen Mary's Dolls' House--Juvenile fiction. 2. Dollhouses--England--Juvenile fiction. 3. Great Britain--History--19th century--Juvenile fiction. 4. Dollhouses--Fiction. 5. Great Britain--History--19th century--Fiction. I. Title.

PS3553.A758 S58 2005
813.6/083

Printed in the United States of America, 2006

Publishing Consultant: Linda F .Radke
Editor: Cathy Fishel
Editor: Thomas Christian Carpenter
Project Manager: Sue DeFabis
Cover Design: Brian Higgins
Book Design: Brian Higgins
Flower Design: Laura Nalesnick

"Come with me and you'll be in a world of pure imagination.
Take a look and you'll see into your imagination...
There is no life I know to compare with pure imagination.
Living there, you'll be free, if you truly wish to be."

From the song "Pure Imagination"
by Leslie Bricusse and Anthony Newley
in the 1971 movie Willie Wonka and the Chocolate Factory

DEDICATION

This book is dedicated to the beauty and power of imagination.
May children everywhere discover and enjoy the creative magic
that is always within their own minds. And may they
hold onto that magic as they grow older.

Contents

Acknowledgments

Many thanks to Eunice Shanahan, of Queensland, Australia.
Eunice was most helpful regarding the details of the postmarks referred to in
The Mystical Dollhouse. Eunice, a regular contributor
to Stamp News Australia, immediately appreciated the importance
of accuracy, and assisted by researching the postmarks as they
would have appeared on the letters that are a part of this story.
These postmarks, as you will learn, helped the Slumber Girls
in their search for answers.

Preface

The old woman sat on the blue-gray upholstered window seat of her room, looking out at what would be the last warm day of the year. Her stiff hands gently cupped a small something, a very special something.

A breeze, cooled by the oncoming evening, lifted a strand of her long, white hair away from the thick twist at the back of her head. She took no notice, but lifted the object in her hand to her cheek for just a moment. She did not have to look at it: Every stitch, every tiny pearl, every carved detail was in her memory already. It was to this day, nearly 65 years since she received it, still the most precious and astounding gift anyone had ever given her.

She read it in the paper this morning. Her very best friend and closest confidant since she was a teenager had passed away. That they had only met one time seemed as much a miracle as what she held in her hand.

As she had done before at least a thousand times since she was a young girl, she tenderly placed the object in the center of the thick square of dark violet velvet lying in her lap and wrapped it carefully. Then she gently placed the gift back in its wooden box and closed its lock.

“Sleep tight,” she said to no one in particular. “It’s time for someone else to dream about you.”

And she never opened the box again.

Chapter One
An Unexpected Clue

"Maya! You have to promise!" insisted Prisi.

"But I don't understand. What's the big secret? Please, please, please, tell me!" asked Maya, clasping her graceful fingers beneath a dramatically pushed out chin. As usual, she had arrived late and had not a clue as to what was going on. "You didn't steal it or anything. It just fell out of a book? Right?"

MaiTae, Skye and Prisi stood in the huge library of Prisi's two-story brick house, hands on hips like three solemn, fashionably dressed guards. Then MaiTae's dimples appeared as she smiled at Maya's earnest pleading, and soon the others were smiling, too. It was hard to stay mad at Maya for long.

"No, of course not, I didn't steal anything," said Prisi. "But we're probably not supposed to do what we're about to do."

"Huh?" asked Maya.

Prisi took hold of her wrists. "Maya! You're too funny!" she replied. "Just follow me. But first, you all have to double-dare promise not to tell anyone."

As she waited for their answer, she tried for the hundredth time that day to pin her wildly curly blond hair down with a headband. The girls nodded in agreement. So she put her finger to her lips.

"Shhh," she cautioned, a tiny smile on the corners of her lips. "Let's go."

It had all begun innocently enough. Three of the four Slumber Girls—for that's what they liked to call themselves due to all of the sleepover parties and dreams that they had shared—had spent that Saturday morning alternately lying on their backs and their stomachs in the cool grass of Prisi's backyard, bathed in the shadows of a giant sugar maple tree while sharing their dreams for the upcoming summer vacation.

MaiTae broke the peace. She groaned, stretched, and announced that she needed to go to the library.

"I have to write a one-page paper about England," she said. "It's due on Monday, and I haven't even started yet."

"Oh, you can't leave now," begged Prisi, who had plans to discuss the upcoming issue of *The Slumber Girls Gazette*, a small newspaper that the girls published periodically with Prisi's dad, the editor of the *Highland Park Post.* "Maya should be here any minute. My mom says you can all stay for lunch."

"But..."

"Besides," Prisi continued, smoothing the front of her new, bright pink T-shirt, "you can do your homework right here. My dad has almost as many books as the Highland Park

Library. Let's check there first. If you can't find what you need, then you can go to the library. Okay?"

It was true. Prisi's dad did have hundreds and hundreds of books in the library at the front of their big house. Its dark, shiny wood shelves in the library ran from the floor up to a very high ceiling and all around the room. Every shelf was crammed with books.

A ladder, nearly four times as tall as even MaiTae, the tallest of the four friends, was the only way to reach the books on the upper shelves. Made of the same dark, polished wood as the bookshelves, the ladder was connected at the top to a metal track that ran around the room. At the bottom of the ladder were metal wheels that allowed it to be pushed effortlessly along the walls of books.

The ladder was a terrible temptation: In fact, a couple of weeks ago, the girls had taken turns riding the ladder and pushing each other around and around the room as fast as they could go. And although they tried hard to hold in their giggles, Prisi's mother had been working in the garden just outside of the library window. She came in to investigate and found four pretty girls looking very guilty indeed.

"We're allowed to look at any book we want," said Prisi. "Only we can't, you know…"

The three girls covered their smiles with cupped palms and nodded. They opened the big double doors to the library. The smells of a fireplace, leather and old paper greeted them instantly. Despite the fun they had there, entering the room always caused the girls to go quiet. Even Maya, who had something to say about everything, was always awestruck.

"There you go, MaiTae. I'm sure you can find something here," said Prisi. She pushed the ladder toward her friend, and it rolled to a stop in front of her. MaiTae tilted her head to look up, and her long, thick black pigtails streamed down her back.

"Hold the ladder," she asked her friends, "so it doesn't…you know."

Prisi and Skye each took hold of a side of the ladder, and their friend climbed slowly up. Skye absentmindedly began humming a song she had been writing.

On the third row from the ceiling, MaiTae spotted several books about England.

"Here's one," she said, pointing to a large, old and obviously heavy book. Stamped in gold leaf on a rich red leather cover was the title, *The Complete History of the English Empire.*

"Complete history? Well, that should certainly do it," said MaiTae. She reached for the book, and on tiptoe, started to coax it with her strong fingers toward the edge of the shelf. Finally, its weight tipped heavily into her palm and at the very same instant, she saw something shiny slip from the pages of the book.

"Look out!" she shouted.

They all watched, frozen in place, as the object tumbled end over end in what seemed like slow motion and finally hit the floor with a metallic clink. Then it was perfectly silent.

Chapter Two
A Key to the Past

MaiTae scurried down the ladder and fell to her hands and knees with the other girls. They frantically searched everywhere for whatever had fallen—behind lamps, under the chair, around the ladder.

"What was it? Where is it?" breathed Skye, her olive cheeks blushing with excitement.

A worried little frown had appeared on Prisi's forehead. She still hadn't worked off all of the chores that had been given to her after the ladder incident.

"I don't know, but we have to find it and put it back," she whispered.

"Here it is!" squealed MaiTai, emerging from behind a large painted vase that was bigger than she was. In her right hand was a two-inch-long piece of formed brass: a very old key.

"Let's see it," said Prisi.

They all took turns holding the key and examining it from every angle.

"What do you think it opens?" asked Skye.

"I don't know, but it must be something old, and it must be something that somebody didn't want anybody to find. I think we should put it back in the book and put the book away."

"What about my homework?" MaiTae asked. "Can't we put everything back later?"

"Yes, I suppose so," said Prisi, her curiosity growing faster than her dread of more chores. "If we're not going to put it back right now, why don't we see what it opens?"

Quietly, so as not to draw the attention of Prisi's mother, who was once again tending her purple Siberian iris right outside the window, the girls began to try the key in all of the doors and drawers of the library. None were even close to being the right locks. The key was much older than anything in the room.

"The attic!" whispered Prisi, her freckles now very clear on her excited face.

"What attic?" asked MaiTae, instantly interested in a new investigation.

"That's where the lock that goes with this key has to be. It's like a museum up there."

At that moment, the door swung open and the bright light of the hallway spilled into the room. The three girls in the library jumped in fright. Prisi's hands were shaking as she tried to hide the key behind her back.

"Hey, Slumber Girls, what's up?" grinned Maya.

"You nearly gave us heart failure!" whispered MaiTae, hands on hips. "Quick, shut the door."

"What did I do? What's going on?" Maya stopped smiling and looked confused.

The girls quickly filled her in on everything that had happened that morning and told her what they planned to do next. They agreed to Prisi's double-dare promise to not share this secret with anyone else. They all put their hands together and looked into each other's eyes.

"Slumber Girls forever?" asked Prisi.

"Slumber Girls forever!" all four shouted in unison.

Chapter Three
A Discovery in the Attic

The girls opened the door to the attic at the end of the upstairs hallway and slowly began to climb the stairs. Every time a tread creaked, they all froze, listening to make sure no one heard them.

"This is creepy," whispered MaiTae, brushing cobwebs away from her face. "Did I ever mention that I hate spiders?"

"Yes, only about a million times since we started going up the stairs," Maya hissed back, aiming the small flashlight she had pulled out of her backpack toward her friend's worried, long-lashed eyes. "Do you want me to go first?"

"Keep your voices down, OK?" said Prisi in a low tone. "There is no way that we are supposed to be up here."

At the top of the stairs there was another door. MaiTae turned the doorknob with a sweaty hand, and it opened with a long and seemingly endless creak.

"I'm not sure this is such a good idea after all," said MaiTae. "My stomach hurts."

"Mine, too," answered Maya. "But we're here. We might as well go on, now." She aimed her small light into the windowless darkness. The other girls groped with their hands along the walls, searching for a light switch that was not there.

Skye found a very old pull cord that led to a bare bulb in the ceiling. It broke off with a brittle snap when she pulled it, but not before the stuffy room was flooded with light. The girls all inhaled as if they were one person.

The attic was filled with very old things that Prisi had never dreamed were in her house, directly over her bedroom. In one corner, there were several old oil paintings of elegantly dressed women. One painting was much larger than the rest.

"Wow, would you look at that," wondered Skye. She knelt in front of the large painting, drawn in by its sweeping paint strokes, by the silky fabric of the woman's clothes and her twist of beautiful white hair. "Who do you suppose she is?"

Nobody was listening, though. Each of the other three girls was lost in her own thoughts and discoveries.

"This isn't an attic," said Maya, "It is a museum!" Everywhere they looked were antique rocking chairs, stacks of old books, statues, paintings, and even an old dressmaker's dummy with swatches of rich, embroidered cloth fixed to it with pearl-topped hat pins.

In one corner was a stack of trunks, several large and one small. "Prisi, look at these!" said MaiTae with a smile. "These all have old locks!"

Prisi still clutched the key in her hand. She looked at the other girls, and they all tiptoed over to the stack. Prisi tried the key in the first two trunks: The key was too small for either. She tried the next trunk: This time the key fit the lock, but would not turn. She held her breath for just a second—only one trunk left, a small one that had obviously traveled many miles in the past. It was scarred with years of use and covered with stickers from Egypt, England, India, and New York City, as well as with luggage tags from ocean liners that the girls had read about in their history books.

She slipped the key into the lock: It fit. Ever so slowly, she turned the key to the left. Nothing. Then she turned it to the right. With a soft click, the lock popped open. Prisi's eyes were as bright green as her friends had ever seen as she stared at their surprised faces.

"Open it!" said Maya. "I can't stand it anymore!"

"It has to have something valuable inside," said MaiTae. "Probably a painting by a famous artist!"

"No, no, I think it's jewels," dreamed Skye. "Pearls or diamonds or gold or—a big ruby!"

Prisi placed the small trunk in the center of the dusty wooden floor so they could all peer inside. The friends gathered around, and Prisi held her breath as she lifted the lid.

Chapter Four
A Flower in the Corner

Inside the small trunk was no painting, no jewels, nothing the girls expected. Instead, Prisi reached inside to retrieve stacks and stacks of letters, each bundle tied together with a wide, faded red satin ribbon. The girls sat in silence, feeling more than a little disappointed.

Prisi felt around inside the box. "Wait! There's something else in here."

Using both hands, she pulled out a wooden box—a plain wooden box with what appeared to be a crown carved in the lid.

"Jewels!" exclaimed Skye, reaching out a finger to trace the carving on the box.

"Not so loud!" Prisi hissed. "We're not supposed to be here! Remember?"

More guesses were quickly traded, and when everyone was again quiet, Prisi lifted the lid off of the box. She carefully pulled away a blanket of deep, purple velvet. Inside was absolutely the last thing the girls expected to see: a small, four-poster, canopy bed from a dollhouse. But it was not an ordinary piece of dollhouse furniture. This was the most intricately, most detailed bed the girls had ever seen in their lives, small or large.

It was complete down to the tiniest of details and was obviously very old. The bedcover was made of shiny blue-gray silk, and it was quilted with hundreds of the tiniest pearls. The stitching on the canopy was so delicate and fine that it looked as though fairies had wielded their needles at it for many months. The canopy on the bed with its four pairs of long drapes made the bed taller than it was wide or long. A very tiny person could jump on the bed and still not touch its elaborate carved roof.

"What is it? I mean, I know what it is, but why is it here?" asked Maya.

"I have no idea," said Prisi slowly and in absolute wonder as she gently set the bed on top of the small trunk lid. "But I'll bet these letters will tell us." She reached for a bundle, untied it, and studied the letters. Each was addressed in a deep purple ink and written in a flowing script, much more elaborate than the cursive the girls had been taught in school. In the lower left-hand corner of each envelope was a small, hand-drawn picture of a flower. Each letter was addressed to a Mary Ballantine.

"Who is Mary Ballantine?" Skye asked Prisi. "Your grandmother?"

"No, my grandmother's name was Margaret. I have no idea who Mary Ballantine was or is."

"Ask your mom!" insisted Maya.

"I can't! Then she'll know we've been snooping around in the attic. We're not even supposed to be up here. We'd better go before we get in trouble."

She spread the purple velvet cloth in her lap, placed the unbelievable bed in the center, and rewrapped it carefully. She noticed a long, white hair clinging to the cloth. But before she had a chance to consider where it came from, a sharp voice rang up the stairs.

"Priscilla Anne Ballantine! Get down here this instant!"

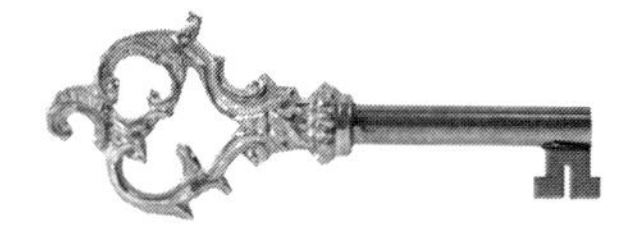

Chapter Five
The Woman in the Painting

"We'd better get going," said the girls as they quickly repacked the trunk and made a beeline toward the front door.

"Don't worry," said Skye, patting Prisi's shoulder as she left. "I'll call you later."

Prisi's mother had spotted the open attic door. Once the other girls were gone, she faced her very guilty-looking daughter.

"I'm sorry, Mom," she blurted out before her mother could say a word. "We were just exploring. I know I should have asked you first." She didn't say anything about the key or the trunk or the letters or the bed. She also didn't wait for her mother to begin scolding.

"Mom, who are all of those women in the paintings up there?" she asked, trying to steer the conversation away from the chance of being assigned chores as punishment. An only child, Prisi had all of her parents' attention all of the time—which was great for fun times like birthdays, but not so great when punishments were doled out.

"I don't know all of them," her mother answered, "but they're all from your father's side of the family. They had wonderful old names like Margarite, Eunice, Beatrice—old-fashioned names like those. The woman in the big painting is your great-great-great grandmother Ballantine."

"What was her first name?

Her mother thought a moment. "I'd have to look it up to make certain, but I believe her name was Mary. Mary Ballantine."

Chapter Six
Mary Meets Mary

Getting through the next day at school was impossible. The girls could not stop thinking about the letters and the little bed. At lunch, they finally had a minute to all sit together and talk some more. MaiTae, Skye and Maya begged Prisi to go back to the attic.

"I don't know," said Prisi, nervously twisting a strand of already curly hair into an almost knot. She had a close call with her mother yesterday. "I don't think it's a very good idea."

The other three girls all stared at her silently: Prisi couldn't be serious. They hadn't even read a single letter.

"Did you get in big trouble?" asked Skye sympathetically.

Prisi shook her head. "Noooo, but I'm not sure we should push our luck."

"Did your mom say to stay out of the attic?" asked Maya.

"Noooo, she didn't say that."

"So can we go back?" asked MaiTae.

"Okay, okay," sighed Prisi. "But we are going to get in trouble. I just know it."

As soon as school was out, the four friends rushed to Prisi's house. They pretended to spend time with the pink lemonade and brownies her mother had left out for a snack, then rushed upstairs, up the attic stairs, and tiptoed back to the small trunk. MaiTae removed from her backpack a flashlight, a three-foot-long piece of twine, and a glow-in-the-dark ball. She tied one end of the twine to the broken end of the light fixture string and the other end to the ball.

"There," she said, satisfied. "Now we'll always be able to find the string to turn on the light."

"You are amazing," declared Maya. "Is there anything you don't have in that bag?"

The Slumber Girls sat down on the attic floor and waited as Prisi placed the small trunk in the center of their circle. She removed a chain from around her neck that held the old key. Finally, she took a deep breath and unlocked the trunk. After raising the lid, she removed the bundles of letters and the carefully wrapped dollhouse bed. The four girls sat solemnly looking at the objects that had completely taken over their curiosity.

"Where do we start?" asked Skye.

Prisi picked up one of the bundles of letters and studied their postmarks. "All the letters in this pile are from London," she said.

"So are these letters," said Maya, examining another bundle.

"These are, too," said MaiTae.

All but a few of the letters were from London. "I can't read these postmarks because they're blurred, but the stamps look like they're from Italy," said Skye, who had a knack for reading and understanding just about any language or music. "And these are addressed to Mary Cambridge, not Mary Ballantine. Who's that?"

"I don't know. But these letters are to Mary Cambridge, too," noted Prisi.

"Not these," said Skye. "My letters are all addressed to Mary Ballantine."

"I know that is my great-great-great-grandmother," answered Prisi. She studied her letters again. "You know what? Look at the postmarks. These letters were mailed in 1884. They are way old. They're antiques!"

The girls soon discovered that the letters were tied together according to the years in which they were sent, and so they lined up the bundles in order of oldest to the most recent. In all, there were nine bundles, and the last letter was mailed in 1949. Skye noticed that all of the oldest letters were mailed to Mary Cambridge. After 1893, all of the letters were to Mary Ballantine. They concluded that both Marys must be the same person: Ballantine was her married name. But it was clear that the letters were all from one person: same handwriting, same purple ink, same flower in the lower corner.

"I wish my handwriting was that good," said MaeTai. "Whoever wrote these must have practiced a lot."

"Are we ready to begin?" asked Prisi, lifting the oldest bundle. The girls nodded eagerly. Slowly and with dramatic flair, she wiped the perspiration from her hands and untied the first pile. She removed the letter from the top envelope and began reading.

10 August 1884
Dearest Mary,

I cannot thank you enough for introducing yourself to me at the Palatine Gallery in the Pitti Palace a few weeks ago. I'm only sorry that we didn't have more time to get to know one another before those horrid men hurried me off like that. They work for my father who's hired them to escort me wherever I go. They mean well, as does he, I'm certain. It's just that they hardly ever give me time by myself. At this rate, I'll never have any friends of my own, much less a husband some day.

It was such a beautiful day the day I met you, Mary Cambridge. I shall remember it forever. It was Tuesday, the fifteenth of July, and it was an absolutely glorious summer day. The sun was shining and the air was warm and dry. It was such a welcome relief from the unseasonably cold and rainy weather we'd been having here in Florence.

I realize you know so little about me, and I know so little about you. Allow me to go first and give you some of the "tantalizing" details of my life, most of which I have no doubt you will find excruciatingly boring.

My father moved my family (my mother and my younger brothers and I) from our beautiful home in London, England, last year. It seems we were experiencing some financial difficulties. I'm too embarrassed to go into the details here, and it probably would not be proper for me to do so. Regardless, the result was that we simply could not stay in England any longer, and so we packed up what we needed, stored the rest, and took our leave. For the next several months, we traveled through Europe, staying with friends and family whenever possible.

We finally found a place we could call our own in Florence, Italy, and so have settled into a villa here for a while. We all do hope, however, that we can soon return to London. But how happy I am that I was in Florence, otherwise I would not have had the pleasure of meeting you.

I absolutely adore visiting art galleries, as I think I mentioned to you when we met. I had been shopping (a talent that I seemingly acquired from my mother) for most of the day that Tuesday, and father's assigned men were complaining that their feet were sore. We were walking down Piazza Pitti, and there we were in front of my favourite gallery.

The reason I love it so is that, as you discovered for yourself, it is more a palace than a formal art gallery. In fact, for some time it was the Palazzo Pitti—the palace home of the Pitti family. They were the grand dukes of Tuscany, I believe. I have always felt that I was born to live in such a palace. Perhaps I will someday.

My father's men were much relieved to find that I simply wanted to sit and gaze at the paintings by Raphael. They were more interested in sitting and sleeping than in looking at the artwork or, as it turns out, than in watching me. I am so glad that you came and sat next to me on that bench. Yes, we share the same name, but something within me makes me believe we share so much more than that.

I told you that my name, too, was Mary. What I didn't share with you was my full name. I hope you're prepared for this. My given name is Victoria Mary Augusta Louise Olga Pauline Claudine Agnes May. Some people call me Mary, while others call me May. Unless someone also calls you May (or Victoria or Augusta or Louise or Olga or Pauline or Claudine or Agnes), let's simply agree to call one another Mary. Does that please you?

"Wow," said Prisi, putting the letter in her lap. "I always thought that Priscilla Anne Ballantine was a mouthful. I wonder why she had so many names."

"Keep on reading, Priscilla Anne Ballantine," urged Maya with a smile. Prisi stuck her tongue out at her, and then picked up the letter and continued reading.

> So, dear Mary, I'm afraid that I've rambled on far too long about myself. I am so curious to learn more about you. What brought you to Florence, Italy? How did you happen to be in the Palatine Gallery that day? What prompted you to introduce yourself to me? Tell me about your family, your friends, where you go to school. I simply want to know everything. Is that too much to ask? If you could see me now, you would see that I am smiling and so happy to have you as a friend.
>
> I will close for now and anxiously await the arrival of your response. Do remember to draw the flower in the lower left-hand corner of the envelope, as I have done. I do hate to sound so mysterious. It's just that so much of my life is controlled by others. I will instruct everyone that they are not to open any envelope bearing the picture of that flower, but rather they are to deliver it to me personally and without delay.
>
> Be well, my dear new friend.
> With warmest regards from Italy,
> *Princess Mary of Teck*

"Princess Mary!" exclaimed Prisi. "My great-great-great grandmother's best friend was a princess?"

"What or where is Teck?" asked Maya. No one knew.

"Wow, that explains the little flowers on all the envelopes," said MaiTae. "Do you think she was being held prisoner in a castle tower or something? You know, like Rapunzel?"

"How could she be a prisoner if she's out shopping and going to art galleries?" asked Skye.

"I thought I had a lot of questions before I read that letter," said Prisi. "Now I have thousands."

"Read another one, Prisi," urged Maya. "Yeah, another one," chimed in the others.

Prisi started to open another envelope, but then looked at her watch. "Yikes! We have a soccer game in 30 minutes! We're supposed to meet our parents there."

In a flurry combined with lots of regret, they retied the bundle of letters and returned them all, along with the dollhouse bed, to the small trunk in the corner.

"Princess Mary," whispered Skye to herself as she fingered the carving of the crown on the smallest box. "Who are you? Where are you?"

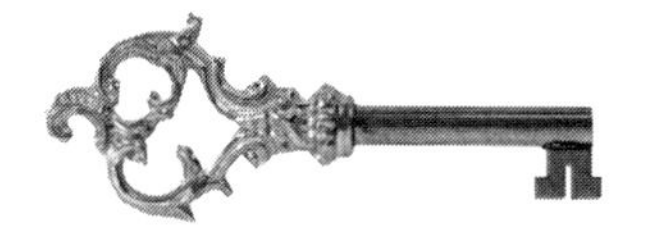

Chapter Seven
A Royal Connection

"The Queen! She's the Queen!"

Prisi was almost shrieking as she ran down the school hallway toward her friends, who stood speechless.

"What are you talking about?" asked Maya. "Stop, stop—calm down! Who's the Queen?"

"Princess—Mary—of—Teck!" gasped Prisi, trying to catch her breath. "She became Queen Mary! She became the Queen of England!"

Her friends clapped their hands over their mouths for a second, then all began to talk at once. Maya jumped up and down in place, her brown hair swinging like a shiny wave.

Skye grabbed Prisi's hand. "Your great-great-great grandmother was best friends with the Queen of England!"

"I know," said Prisi. "Can you believe it? Let's go. We've got to find out more."

* * *

"Priscilla Ballantine thinks she is going to be the queen," snorted Rebecca Rodgers to her friend Abigail Lukens. Both girls leaned sulkily on their lockers. "I just overheard her talking to her friends. We have to do something to stop her."

Everyone knew that Rebecca Rodgers felt that only she deserved to be Highland Park Middle School's Queen for a Day. Each year right before school let out for the summer, Dr. Stewart Livingston, the principal, would pick one boy student and one girl student to be King and Queen for a Day.

Being selected for this honor meant that absolutely everybody in the whole town knew you were somebody special, and Rebecca was convinced that there was no one more special than she. Never mind that the honor was meant to recognize students who had made a significant contribution to their school and community during the year. As far as Rebecca Rodgers was concerned, she was born to be at least Queen for a Day. After all, hadn't she written a letter to the editor praising Dr. Livingston, the school's principal? She had gone on and on about what a wonderful job he was doing at Highland Park Middle School. She had written about how he'd inspired her to volunteer for a whole hour at the homeless shelter.

"I don't believe that," said Abigail. "Sure, Prisi likes to run things, but she's never seemed interested in being Queen for a Day. What did she say, anyway?"

"I don't know," said Rebecca. "It was more how she said it than what. I also heard Skye Lee say something to MaiTae Marshall about her being the queen's best friend. What else could it mean?"

"Do you want me to ask her?" said Abigail.

"Oh, now that's really, really smart. Then she'll know that we know what she's up to. No. We just have to put our heads together and come up with some way to stop her, that's all."

That afternoon, the Slumber Girls again met secretly in the attic of Prisi's house. They agreed to take turns, each girl reading the letters contained in a bundle.

Prisi began untying the bundle that contained the letter she'd read yesterday. She checked the postmarks to make sure the letter she was about to read was the next one that Mary Cambridge had received.

The four girls were soon once again engrossed with the story of friendship and dreams that rang so true to them. It was like a fairy tale come true.

There were two more letters from 1884, the year Mary Cambridge had met Princess Mary. The girls learned that the young princess loved art and so she visited art galleries wherever she and her family traveled. In the second letter, Princess Mary wrote to her new friend telling her a bit more about herself. "Listen to this part," said Prisi.

I don't much like people staring at me, Mary. I don't imagine anyone does. Anyway, I do my best to ignore them. What happens though is that people—especially people who don't know me very well—think that I'm either shy or rude.

I'll admit I don't often smile when I'm around strangers. But ask my brothers and they'll tell you that I'm not like that at all. Tell me what you're like; would you do that for me?

"That sounds a little like you, doesn't it?" Prisi said, looking at Skye. She blushed.

When Prisi finished reading the second letter, she carefully folded it and slipped it back into the envelope. "This next one is the last letter she got that year." She took the third letter from its envelope and began reading.

1 December 1884
Dearest Mary,

So we do share more than simply our names. I just knew it. The way you described yourself in your last letter made it sound as though you were writing about me.

I find our whole friendship so utterly fascinating, don't you? We have so much in common, probably more than we know. I will begin keeping note of the things we share in common.

First, although they are not the same dates, when I tell you when I was born, you will have to admit that our birthdays are nearly close enough to call us twins. Our birthdays are not even separated by a whole month. You said you were born on 15 April 1867. I was born on 26 May that very same year. So we are both 17 years old now. I wish we'd known each other all the years before now. I have little doubt that we could have invented great games of fun and mischief together.

Now do sit down before you read what I have to say next. We are finally going home. Father made the announcement at dinner last evening. It seems that all the financial difficulties have been resolved and we are returning to London after the first of the year.

We have been given a place to stay in London. Granted, it is not the palace or castle to which I believe myself to have been born. It is, nonetheless, a most comfortable home. Unless you write back to me right away, I think it best if you addressed your next letter to me at the White Lodge in Richmond Park. That address should be sufficient.

White Lodge is an old home (but isn't everything in England?). Father says it was built in 1729 for King George II. I always loved visiting Richmond Park when I was a child. It has great oak forests. I was convinced they were enchanted forests, and they very well might be, for it hasn't been proven otherwise. It has thousands of acres of lakes and streams and hills and grassy fields, in addition to the ancient woodlands. I do hope you can persuade your family to make a trip to England so that you can see it (and me, of course). Richmond Park absolutely abounds with deer and other wildlife. I shall enjoy living there, I feel certain, while I wait for the palace of my dreams.

With great fondness,
Princess Mary

As if on cue, all four girls sighed in unison.

MaiTae had the next six letters, all from 1885. The girls soon learned a great deal more about Princess Mary of Teck. They read all about her move to White Lodge in Richmond Park, just a short distance southwest of downtown London, England. Princess Mary wrote about how close she was to her mother and how she loved helping her organize grand parties for friends and family.

Maya read her bundle next, and then Skye. They were full of clever stories of fine clothing and fancy dinners, of tricks the princess and her not-always-prince-like brothers played on each other and on servants. Some letters sounded sad, as the princess wrote about how world events were affecting her country and people. Others were full of questions for her American friend about boyfriends and school.

The letters had tapered off to about two or three a year. By the time they were done reading for the afternoon, the Slumber Girls read how Princess Mary had congratulated Mary Cambridge on her marriage on June 10, 1893, to a newspaper publisher by the name of Joseph Gallagher Ballantine—hence, the name change in the address.

"These two really did share a lot in common," said Skye. "Listen to this." She read a letter from Princess Mary describing her elaborate wedding in which she married Prince George, the Duke of York. The descriptions of Mary's wedding dress were so detailed that each girl could picture the rich, white satin brocade, woven with real silk and silver thread, and adorned with sweet-smelling ropes of orange blossoms and the lace from her mother's wedding dress. They could only imagine what it would be like to married in a diamond crown and a necklace with jewels as big as cherries.

"Princess Mary got married just a month after Mary Cambridge did," exclaimed Skye. "It's almost like they were twins." The Slumber Girls continued to be fascinated when they learned that the two women also had their children at about the same time.

They read how Princess Mary became Her Royal Highness, the Princess of Wales, and later Queen Mary when her husband became King George V. That was in 1910. In a letter written four years later, Queen Mary told of the dark storm of war that was sweeping across the European continent. Soon, England was involved. She wrote of how she and her husband were doing everything they could to help win the war. The battles lasted many years, ending finally in November 1918. "You know what," said Prisi, looking at all the letters that lay on the floor in front of her. "I don't think my great-great-great-grandmother ever saw Queen Mary again. It looks to me as though their whole friendship started in that art gallery and all the rest of it was through these letters. I think that's kind of sad."

"I think it's amazing," said Maya. "Even though they couldn't see each other again, they stayed good friends."

"What I think is amazing is how she went from being a young girl in a family with no money to being the Queen of England and living in Buckingham Palace," declared MaiTae. "I mean, think about it. What a great story this is."

Prisi, Skye, MaiTae, and Maya lost all track of time as they sat there reading letter after letter. And just when they thought that nothing else could possibly amaze them, a letter written in the summer of 1922 threw their imaginations into overdrive.

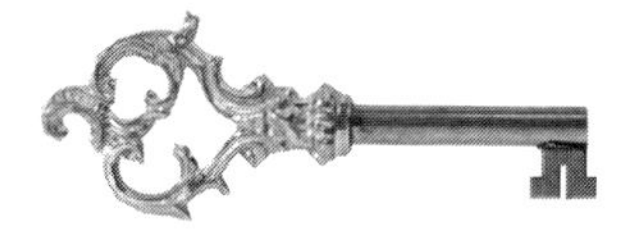

Chapter Eight
Not Just Any Dollhouse

27 August 1922
Dearest Mary,

So much has happened since I last wrote that I'm not certain where to begin. I am now fifty-five years old (as are you, dear friend, can you believe it?), and I am about to receive a gift of a dollhouse. Yes, you read correctly, I am being given a dollhouse. This, briefly, is the story.

It all started on Easter a year ago. My husband's cousin, Princess Mary Louise, was visiting us and was struck by a most remarkable and unusual idea. She knows how much I love collecting miniature figurines, tiny furniture, and other small items—"tiny craft" we call them here. If you were ever to grace us with a visit, I would love to show them to you. I am embarrassed to say that I have gone a bit overboard with my passion for miniatures. My collections fill so many glass cabinets that, quite honestly, I've lost count. Somehow, Princess Mary Louise got it in her head that I needed a dollhouse. At my age!

She didn't tell me at first, instead choosing to talk to Sir Edward Lutyens, one of the foremost architects of our time. Sir Lutyens is in the midst of an enormous undertaking, as he is in charge of designing more than eighty square miles of offices and palaces in New Delhi, India. He is creating an entire city, and Princess Mary Louise was so bold as to ask if he would, at the same time, design for me a dollhouse.

He said he would. Is that not incredible?

Mary, we have already held several meetings on the project and it is developing into something extraordinarily grand. It will be a dollhouse like none other. We have decided to use it to show the world the wonderful talents of our English artisans. It is my sincere hope that the world will take note, for our economy suffered greatly during the war. Our many industries could certainly use the good publicity it is my hope this dollhouse will generate.

The current plans call for the dollhouse to contain more than forty rooms on four floors. Sir Lutyens has designed it to include two staircases, hot and cold running water in each of the five bathrooms with toilets that actually flush, two lifts (elevators, I believe you call them in the United States), and electric chandeliers and lights that you can turn on and off with little switches on the walls. I sometimes think the dear man has begun to lose touch with reality.

It goes without saying that I am quite excited about this project. I will be certain to write more as the work progresses. Meanwhile, be safe and be happy, my dear friend.

With warmest regards,
Mary

"That has to be the most expensive dollhouse in the history of the whole world," exclaimed Maya, putting the letter back into the envelope. "This bed has to be from that house, don't you think?"

The girls knew there was only one way to find out, and so they continued reading. A few letters later, they found out what they wanted to know, and more. It was Prisi's turn to read.

15 September 1925
Dearest Mary,

I do so apologize for my tardiness in responding to your last letter. I hope all is well with you and Joseph and your precious grandson Gerald Arthur. Thank you so much for the photograph; what a handsome young man he is. Is it possible he's almost two years old already? You must be so proud.

I hope you don't think me obsessed with this dollhouse about which I've written you over the past couple of years. It's just that it blossomed into such an enormous project.

The good news is that it is finally completed and has been on display for the past several months. It was recently shipped to Windsor Castle where it shall remain. It took, I am told, more than 1,500 craftsmen three full years to complete not only the house itself, but also all the absolutely remarkable miniature furnishings. The house and everything in it is built on a scale of one inch per foot. Imagine the skill with which these artisans created all the furniture, paintings, and decorations. Everything is accurately rendered, down to the smallest of details.

The dollhouse library has over 200 books, all done by our most noted authors (some of them even wrote them in their own hand). Similarly, the paintings that hang on the walls of the rooms were painted by England's most famous artists. Dear Mary, I could go on and on. I'll enclose a newspaper article which contains even more information about this astonishing creation.

Now to the real purpose of this letter to you. Shortly, you will be receiving from me a package. It is important, for reasons I am about to explain to you, that you keep this gift a secret between the two of us. I know you will, as you have always kept our correspondence private. What a comfort it is to have a friend like you!

When the dollhouse arrived at Windsor Castle, I promptly examined every room of it. I discovered that the bed in the Queen's bedroom had been damaged somehow. I pointed it out to Sir Edward Lutyens, the architect in charge of every aspect of the project. Instead of offering to repair it, he immediately

ordered a replacement bed be made. When the replacement bed arrived, I switched it with the damaged bed.

I never mentioned to anyone what I did with the original bed, and so everyone assumed I had destroyed it. (I couldn't possibly do that; goodness, it was far too exquisite.) The result is that there are now two such beds for the Queen's bedroom.

I am making a gift to you of the original bed. So, since this bed supposedly no longer exists, please do me the favour of keeping this confidential. Even without asking, I know I can count on you.

This dollhouse bed is yours as a symbol of our friendship that began so many years ago when we were much, much younger. Let it represent our childhoods and lives that we have shared over the years.

Please write me when you receive it and tell me what you think of it. I can only imagine that you'll say, "Who could sleep in such a thing?" Oh, we do get used to the finer things in life, don't we, dear friend?

With warmest regards,
Mary

The girls looked at each other, at the dollhouse bed sitting there on the floor of the attic, and then again at each other. Their mouths were open, but for once, the girls were speechless.

Chapter Nine

From Attic To Stage

"Mom, there's something I've got to tell you."

Prisi and her mother were having fresh fruit salads for dinner by themselves, as her father was working late at his office at *The Highland Park Post.* Prisi took the linen napkin from her lap, folded it, and placed it on the table.

"Yes, Prisi, what is it? Is something wrong?"

"Does something have to be wrong whenever I say that I want to tell you something?"

"No, darling, of course not. So, is something wrong?" She smiled at her pretty daughter.

After a long moment of silence, Prisi began. All in a rush, she told her mother everything—that they had found a key, then a trunk, then the letters and the bed. Everything.

"I'm sorry, Mom. I really am. It's just that once we started reading those letters, we couldn't stop. We wanted to know everything. I know we weren't supposed to be up there snooping around. I'm really, really sorry. I'll do whatever you want. I'll do the dishes for a month. I'll even help with the laundry. I'll do my homework every day—well, maybe every day except Friday—as soon as I come home from school. How long am I going to be grounded?"

"The Queen of England?" Her mother had an astonished look on her face. She clearly was not in punishment mode. "A dollhouse bed from Windsor Castle? Your great-great-great grandmother was best friends with a princess and a queen? Prisi, are you sure about all this?"

"Do you want me to show you?" Prisi asked, greatly relieved. Her mother nodded in a shocked way, and the two of them headed for the attic stairs.

"It's so dark up here, Prisi. Do we need a flashlight?"

"Come with me." Prisi took her mother by the hand and led her to the glow-in-the-dark ball. "Pull it, Mom." She did and the room was flooded with light.

"Is this a MaiTae project?" her mother laughed. Prisi nodded.

Over the next couple of hours, Prisi showed her mother everything. Much like the Slumber Girls were the day before, Prisi's mother was astonished.

"So, Mom, can I play with the dollhouse bed?"

"Oh, I'm not so sure about that, honey. We'll have to ask your father. I'll bet he doesn't know anything about this."

Prisi swallowed hard. "Do you think he'll be mad at me?"

"Well, you didn't break anything and you didn't exactly lie about anything. So, no, I don't think he'll be mad. I do think he'll be as intrigued as we are by all this. Now, young lady, it's off to bed for you. And about washing the dishes every day and doing your homework as soon as you get home? I think that is a great idea."

Prisi groaned as she walked down the stairs. Her mother had heard everything.

"Was she mad at you?"

"Are you grounded or anything?"

"What about the dollhouse bed? Will we ever get to see it again?"

Skye, MaiTae, and Maya kept peppering Prisi with questions as they walked home from school.

"Whoa, slow down," said Prisi. "Everything's all right. She wasn't all that mad with me. I got a few more chores is all. And, yes, I think we can play with the dollhouse bed as long as my mom says it's okay. If you want to know the truth, I think she wants to play with it, too!"

The girls paused on the sidewalk in front of Prisi's house. "Do you want to come in?" she asked. "It's Friday, so I don't have to do my homework until this weekend."

Once inside the elegant, Tudor home, they went into the kitchen to get a snack.

"Mom? What are you doing?"

With a soft, dry paintbrush, Prisi's mother was gently dusting the fabric canopy of the four-poster bed. She looked up and grinned. "You caught me. Yes, I've been playing with the bed. I read the rest of those letters this morning after you went to school. It's a fantastic story. And by the way, I told your father about all this and he wasn't the least bit angry. In fact, he's just as amazed as all of us are."

Then her mother did an amazing thing: She went to the china cupboard and got out the finest cups and saucers and small plates. She brewed some English tea and while it was steeping, she went to the pantry. She came back with a tin of pastry desserts. "These were to be for my book club," she explained, "but they are much more suited for a tea party with the Queen, don't you think?"

What a grand time they had—Princess Prisi of Walnut Street, Lady Skye of Forsythia Circle, Lady Maya of Claxton Lane, Duchess MaiTae of Mayfield Avenue, and of course, Prisi's mother as Queen Marcella of Ballantine—all sitting there wearing feather boas and hats from Prisi's closet, and sipping tea with their pinky fingers extended.

"Do you know what I think I shall do?" Princess Prisi's nose was in the air and she held the teacup daintily in her right hand. "I believe I shall begin doing my homework."

"Are you nuts? I mean, have you gone completely bonkers?" said Lady Skye. "It's Friday afternoon."

"Do tell me more," said Queen Marcella. "Whatever are you thinking?" They all laughed at her horrible British accent.

"Well, you all know that we're each supposed to come up with a special project for Social Studies," said Prisi, removing her favorite green hat. "It's our year-end assignment and it's going to be worth 25 percent of our entire grade."

"I think you need another cookie," said Lady Maya. "You're talking about homework at the Queen's tea party."

"Exactly," said Prisi with a quick nod of her head.

"You're losing me, Prisi. What are you talking about?" asked her mother.

"I think we should put on a play for Social Studies, a play about Princess Mary of Teck and my great-great-great-grandmother. Maybe we could get permission to do it together as a joint project. I'll write the play, with your help, of course. Skye and Maya, you can write some songs for it. And you, MaiTae, can design the sets for the play. We'll call it *The Mystical Dollhouse.* What do you think?"

The girls loved the idea. They divided up jobs, but agreed that all four of them would meet on Monday with Mrs. Robinson, their Social Studies teacher. Together, they would make their plea to Mrs. Robinson for permission work on the project together. She just had to say yes.

"Just like Queen Mary and my great-great-great-grandmother and the dollhouse bed, we have to keep this a complete secret. Okay?"

They all nodded quickly, the flowers and feathers on their hats bobbing in reply.

Chapter Ten
Rebecca Hatches a Plot

"What in the world are you doing, Rebecca?" asked Abigail.

Rebecca was hunkered down on the floor and had her ear pressed against the door to Mrs. Robinson's Social Studies classroom. She motioned for Abigail to be quiet. Abigail knelt down beside her.

"Are you guys okay?" shouted Sylvia Bobine from down the hallway. Sylvia was another of the small but tight circle of friends that hung around Rebecca. Sylvia was friendly enough when she was by herself, but she was quick to assume a bad attitude whenever she was with Rebecca.

"Quiet!" the two girls whispered hoarsely.

"Why? What's up?"

"Would you please be quiet?" insisted Rebecca.

"Okay, okay. But I wish I knew what was going on." Sylvia plopped down on the floor next to them, banging against the classroom door as she did.

"Oh, for crying out loud," said Rebecca as she quickly began gathering up her books. "She heard you—here she comes!"

Rebecca, Abigail, and Sylvia rushed to the other side of the hallway and stood there pretending to be comparing fingernails.

"Well, I'm not sure what that was," said Mrs. Robinson to Prisi, MaiTae, Skye, and Maya, "but I believe we were done anyway. I think the queen idea is a wonderful one. Good luck. I look forward to seeing it happen. But remember, for you to get full credit, it has to be historically accurate." The girls all said they understood.

"Hi, guys," said Prisi as she and the others passed Rebecca and her friends.

Rebecca just stared furiously at them as they walked away.

"Rebecca, will you please tell us what is going on? You are acting so weird," said Sylvia.

"I told you Prisi Ballantine is planning on being Queen for a Day. Now do you believe me?"

"Wow, maybe you were right. What are you going to do?" asked Abigail.

"Before you got here and ruined everything, I heard Prisi telling Mrs. Robinson something about her great-great-great-grandmother being a friend of the Queen of England and that she had the letters to prove it. I guess that somehow makes her think she should be Queen for a Day."

"That's so cool!" exclaimed Abigail before she realized that Rebecca was glaring at her. She quickly tried to cover up her mistake. "I mean, that's so cool that you found out about this, Rebecca."

Rebecca stared at her for a moment before going on. "I think one of you should let somebody know that Prisi is just making it all up. She can't really have letters from the Queen of England."

"Why one of us?" asked Sylvia. "Why don't you do it yourself?"

"Oh, sure, that would work," replied Rebecca. "Everyone knows that I'm the most likely person to be picked for Queen for a Day. They'd just think I'm doing it to make sure I get picked. No, it has to be one of you."

"Ooh, Rebecca, I'm not sure about this," said Sylvia.

"Do it, Sylvia. Otherwise, I just might have to tell Brett that you have a major crush on him."

"Don't you dare!" said Sylvia, her face turning red from embarrassment.

Her blushing seemed to prove it was true. Sylvia did have a crush on Rebecca's brother. Brett was just one year older than they were and was extremely good looking.

"Okay, okay. I'll figure out some way to do it. Just promise me you won't say a word to your brother. I would just die!"

The next day in the cafeteria, Sylvia waited in line to get her food. Then she spotted Miss Wesley, the school counselor, eating lunch by herself in the corner. This is my chance, she thought. After she received her tray, she walked briskly to the counselor's table.

"May I sit here, Miss Wesley?"

"By all means, Abigail. Do join me."

"It's Sylvia, Miss Wesley."

"What?"

"My name is Sylvia. Sylvia Bobine."

"Of course, it is, dear. Why, I know everyone in the school. It's my job, you know."

"Uh-huh." Sylvia rolled her eyes and then took a seat on the bench across from the counselor.

"Miss Wesley, being a school counselor is like being a doctor, right?"

"Well, I suppose you could look at it like that. I try to treat people's problems and make them better. Yes, I guess I am like a doctor. Do you suppose I could get everyone to call me Dr. Wesley?" the counselor joked.

"That's not exactly what I meant, Miss Wesley. Doctors can't tell anyone what their patients tell them, right? I saw that on a TV show. A patient can tell her doctor anything and the doctor has to keep it a secret. Is your job like that? I mean if I tell you something and tell you not to tell anyone I told you, would you? I mean, would you keep my name out of it?"

"Why, of course. Your secret would be safe with me," Miss Wesley assured Sylvia.

Sylvia proceeded to tell Miss Wesley about the letters from the Queen of England that Prisi supposedly had in her possession. "I just know she's making it up. I'd feel bad if

I didn't tell someone before she goes and fools the whole school with this play of hers. I just think someone should stop her for her own sake. I mean, it's a mean prank."

Miss Wesley signed deeply. "Thank you for the courage it must have taken for you to come forward like that," she said. She piled her dishes on her tray and stood up. "I'll see that she doesn't embarrass either herself or Highland Park Middle School."

"Thank you, Miss Wesley."

"Think nothing of it, Skye."

Sylvia didn't correct her this time. She pushed away her food. Her appetite was gone. What have I done?

"Priscilla Ballantine, please report to the office." Hearing one's name on the announcements never meant anything good. Her stomach gave a little jump.

"Priscilla Ballantine," the voice repeated, "please report to the office immediately."

Everyone in her class stared at her as she gathered her books and papers and left the room. It was a long, lonely walk down the deserted hallway. She had no clue what this could be about. As she walked past her locker, she briefly considered hiding in it until school was over. I haven't done anything wrong. What am I afraid of?

When she opened the door to the school office, the secretary said, "Come in, Priscilla, they're waiting for you." She sounded serious.

"Who ..."

"Just come with me." She opened the door to the principal's office.

Inside, Prisi saw Dr. Livingston, Vice Principal Vargas, and Miss Wesley, all seated around a small conference table. "Come in, Priscilla, and have a seat," said Ms. Vargas. Dr. Livingston was nice enough, and the whole school knew how confused Miss Wesley was about most things. But Ms.Vargas? Now she was someone to be afraid of. Ms. Vargas was always on the lookout for troublemakers. Unfortunately, it seemed that Ms. Vargas was in charge of this meeting.

"Miss Ballantine," said Ms. Vargas removing the glasses from the end of her nose and letting them hang from the beaded chain around her neck. "I've been given some disturbing news."

She proceeded to tell Prisi that someone had told them that she'd lied about having in her possession letters from the Queen of England. "Now, Priscilla, fabricating a story like that is bad enough, but to involve your friends? That's quite thoughtless and selfish. Even if you were to produce for us these so-called Queen's letters, how would we know they were real?"

"But ..."

"Please don't interrupt, young lady. Not only are you risking getting an F in Social Studies, you are most likely to cause your friends to fail as well. Now you either drop this whole silly idea or you prove to us beyond a shadow of a doubt that these letters you say you have are real. Do you understand?"

"Yes, ma'am." Prisi was dumbfounded. Someone had spilled the Slumber Girls' secret. Her eyes filled with tears as she realized what kind of trouble she was in.

"Very well then. You may go."

Prisi walked slowly down the corridor. What am I going to do? I want this whole play to be a surprise. Even if I show them the letters, they'll probably think they're not real.

The bell rang and kids poured out of the doorways into the hall.

"Hey, Prisi, wait up!" Maya was running to catch up with her. "What was all that about?"

Prisi told her everything that had just happened. "I don't know what to do," said Prisi. "Part of me wants to keep going and to fight this somehow, but I sure don't want you guys to get hurt in the process."

"Why don't you just have your mom and dad talk to Ms. Vargas?"

"I might," said Prisi, "as a last resort. But they're always so proud of me when I handle things by myself. I started this whole thing and I need to finish it. I just can't imagine who found out about the letters."

As they had planned earlier, Prisi and Maya went to the library where they met up with Skye and MaiTae. They spent the next few hours researching Queen Mary and particularly her dollhouse. Prisi began to feel much better: They were definitely doing the right thing. They found out all kinds of fascinating things. The girls agreed that it was without a doubt the most incredible dollhouse ever made. While Prisi was sitting there at the library table looking at a picture of Queen Mary in the encyclopedia, she had another idea.

Alone in her room later that evening, Prisi got out the box of fancy stationery her grandmother had given her for her last birthday and began writing to Queen Elizabeth, the current Queen of England. She couldn't believe she was doing it, but it might be her only solution.

In her letter, she told the Queen all about her great-great-great-grandmother's letters and even about the dollhouse bed, which she described in much detail. By the third page of the letter, she was telling her all about *The Mystical Dollhouse*, the play she and the other Slumber Girls were writing. She even told her about Ms. Vargas and being called to the principal's office. When she was finished, she read it over more than once to make sure she hadn't made any mistakes. Then she signed it, folded it, and put in an envelope.

"What's her address? How is it going to get to her?" she wondered aloud. Queen Elizabeth, Buckingham Palace, London, England. That should do it. Everyone knows where that is. On a whim, she drew a picture of a small flower in the lower left-hand corner of the envelope.

The next morning, Prisi decided to tell her mother and father everything that had happened at school the day before. They, of course, wanted to get involved and talk to Ms. Vargas. "I can handle this on my own," Prisi said to them. Reluctantly, they agreed.

On her way to school, Prisi took the letter she'd written to the Queen and dropped it in the mailbox on the corner. I sure hope I hear something from her, and fast. A letter from the Queen would prove everything.

Queen Elizabeth, however, would do far more than that.

Chapter Eleven
Better than Proof

In the weeks that followed, the Slumber Girls spent every free moment working on the play, despite the warning from Ms. Vargas. Prisi had finished a rough draft of the script, and Skye and Maya had written some songs especially for the play. MaiTae had been busy, too. She had designed the most wonderful sets for the play. The girls had many weekend slumber parties in which they worked on *The Mystical Dollhouse* late into the night.

Every few days, Ms. Vargas would politely inquire whether Prisi was ready to drop the idea of the play. So far, Prisi had been able to stall her, but she knew that time was running out.

Just one week before the day of the play, an envelope made from the most exquisite paper arrived in the mail. Before she even read the return address, she knew who it was from: in the lower left-hand corner, there was a drawing of a small flower.

Prisi's hands shook as she carried the envelope to her room. She picked up the telephone and called Maya, MaiTae, and Skye. "Get over here right now," she told each of them. "I don't want to tell what it is over the phone, but I've got something important to show you. Just get here!"

Soon, all the Slumber Girls were sitting on Prisi's bed. With great ceremony and with her fingers still shaking, she showed them the envelope postmarked from Buckingham Palace. They gasped when they saw the flower in the corner.

Prisi removed the letter from the envelope and began reading. What the girls heard made their jaws drop. Apparently, the relationship between Prisi's great-great-great-grandmother and Queen Mary was not only very real, it had become part of palace legend, a story passed down from generation to generation. Everyone in the royal family, it seems, knew of the young American girl who had befriended Princess Mary of Teck in her time of need.

She continued to read aloud.

And so, Priscilla, we also knew of the significance of the little flower on the envelope. When your letter to me arrived at Buckingham Palace, my staff didn't know quite what to make of it. Some thought it a hoax, while others believed it could be genuine. They decided not to take a chance with it, and so brought it immediately to me. I shall forever be grateful that they did.

You see, there is more to this than just a remarkable relationship conducted by letters between my grandmother and your grandmother so many years ago. It might just be possible that you and your delightful friends are in a position to help us resolve a lingering mystery here at the palace.

I don't know if the research for your play has uncovered this bit of information yet, but the bed in the princess's bedroom in the dollhouse contained a fairytale surprise. (Are you familiar with the story, "The Princess and the Pea," by Hans Christian Andersen?) Sir Edward Lutyens, the designer of the dollhouse, had a miniature pea placed beneath the mattress of the princess's bed.

Royal rumor has it that in the summer of 1925, one of my grandfather's young nieces and her family were visiting at Windsor Castle. While there, she was given permission to play with my grandmother's dollhouse which had just recently been uncrated. The little girl, who must have been perhaps seven or eight years old at the time, was caught dismantling the princess's bed. She said she was simply looking for the pea to see if the story were true. My grandmother was furious. That little girl got in a lot of trouble for that one.

A few days later, I understand there was an uproar among the royal family and palace staff. A jewel was found to be missing from King Arthur's cup, a goblet that was displayed on a shelf in the main library at Windsor Castle. The goblet supposedly belonged to the legendary King Arthur of England. Embedded in its side was the fabled Ruby of Vidisha, which some say was the twin of the Black Prince's Ruby which adorns the imperial state crown of England. The original source of King Arthur's cup was lost in the pages of history. It was known, however, to have been handed down to the kings and queens of England for centuries. The Missing Ruby of Vidisha, as the newspapers began calling it, was never seen again.

It wasn't until this little girl was a grown woman that she confessed to her mother that she had been playing with that goblet so many years ago. She said it slipped from her hands and fell to the floor, and when it did, the ruby popped out. She said she was trying to stick it back in when some men came into the room. She explained that she quickly replaced the goblet backwards on the shelf, thus hiding the spot where the ruby had been.

Worried that she was going to get in even more trouble, and still a bit peeved with our grandmother for being punished earlier, she compounded her mistake by making another.

She admitted to her mother that she hid the Ruby of Vidisha under the mattress in the Queen's bedroom in the dollhouse. She said, "I felt that the Queen, quite unlike the princess in the fairytale, was so insensitive that she'd never even feel something so large and lumpy as that ruby, much less a pea."

A search of the dollhouse and the Queen's bed within it was conducted almost immediately. No ruby, however, was ever found. When I read your letter, Priscilla, it struck me. Unbeknownst to us till now, there were two beds constructed for the Queen's bedroom in the dollhouse. It is just possible that the Missing Ruby of Vidisha is hidden within the bed that you have discovered.

The letter slipped from Prisi's fingers unnoticed and landed on the bed. "Oh, my stars. I cannot believe what I am reading. If this is true..."

The girls turned and stared at the wood box from the attic. Prisi had placed it on a shelf in her bedroom as inspiration for her while she wrote the play. For the longest time, no one said a word.

"Prisi?" said Maya, her voice quivering. "I think you should get the box." The other girls nodded slowly.

Prisi slid off the bed, walked over to the bookshelf and returned with the box. She put it on the bed in the middle of their circle. She took a deep breath and let it out with a big sigh. "Okay, here goes."

She removed the lid with the carved crown on it and ever so carefully lifted the purple velvet parcel out of the box. She looked at MaiTae, Skye, and Maya. Then she pulled away the thick cloth from the bed and gently removed the covers and then the sheets from the tiny bed. With her finger, she poked at the mattress. "It's hard," she said in a whisper. She took the mattress off the bed and there, stuck tightly in the bed frame, was a rich, red, sparkling gem, as big as a half-dollar coin.

The Missing Ruby of Vidisha was in her bedroom. "Oh, oh, oh," was all that Prisi could muster.

The girls each took a turn holding the jewel in their hands, turning it over and over and marveling at its beauty. "Skye was right," said Maya, holding the jewel up to the light. "The treasure really was a ruby. I can't believe it."

"Let's get back to the letter," said Prisi. "I'm almost to the end."

> If indeed my suspicions prove correct, then you have solved one of the greatest mysteries in the history of the royal family. The Ruby of Vidisha is extremely valuable, and so it is imperative that you tell no one other than your parents. If indeed you do find the ruby, please do me the important favour of giving it to your mother and father for safekeeping, preferably in a bank vault.
>
> Now, I have an offer to make you...

When Prisi finished reading the last two pages of the letter, the girls had goose bumps all up and down their arms. This was the biggest secret yet. How could they possibly keep it to themselves until the night of the play?

Chapter Twelve
Ms. Vargas Persists

"Ms. Vargas, you're just going to have to trust me. Yes, I know. Yes. Yes, I certainly agree that this is a serious issue." Mrs. Ballantine struggled to maintain her composure.

Prisi sat at the kitchen table, watching as her mother tried politely to end the telephone conversation.

"Ms. Vargas, Prisi is a fine student, and the others are, too. She and MaiTae, Maya, and Skye have maintained high grades all year. Really, I do have to... Yes...yes. All right. But, please don't do anything. Let the play go on, and I know you will understand. Everyone will understand. Thank you. Yes, thank you, Ms. Vargas. Good-bye."

She smiled at Prisi. "She's quite convinced that your play is going to embarrass not only you, but the entire school and even the town. Are you sure you don't want to..."

"No, Mom. I'm sure. This way, the *Slumber Girls Gazette* will have the exclusive story. Well, Dad's paper, too, since he prints our paper for us."

For the past two years, Prisi and her friends had produced, with her father's help, a small newspaper called the Slumber Girls Gazette. Prisi, an aspiring author, wrote most of the stories for the paper, and the others contributed, too. MaiTae drew pictures for the paper, Skye wrote a music column called "The Skye's the Limit," and Maya wrote "Maya's Spotlight," articles about fun things to do in Highland Park.

The Slumber Girls Gazette was a lot of fun to put together and this was real news to report. Prisi was writing an article about what would happen the night of the play. She knew it was going to be big news at Highland Park Middle School, and maybe throughout the whole town of Highland Park, too.

She just had no idea just how big it was going to be.

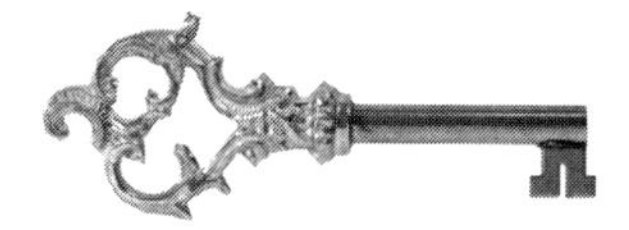

Chapter Thirteen
An Evening to Remember

"What is going on, Prisi?" asked MaiTae.

It was Saturday afternoon, and Prisi and the other Slumber Girls were on their way to the school to make the final arrangements for their play. The opening act of *The Mystical Dollhouse* was only a few hours away.

They were about a block from the school when they saw them—television news trucks from all over were parked around the school. There was even one from the TV station in the state capital, which was nearly three hundred miles away.

"I am not panicking," was all Prisi could say. She said it again. "I am not panicking." Her eyes were wide with wonder. "I...am...not...panicking."

"Well, come on," said Maya. "We have to find out what's going on. Maybe there's been a fire at the school or something."

The four girls took off running. When they got there, they picked their way over the television cables that snaked back and forth across the school's parking lot. One of the news reporters spotted them.

"Hey, it's you, isn't it?" he shouted. He grabbed a microphone, and he and a man with a big camera started to follow them. "Come on, it's you. You're the ones who discovered the Missing Ruby of Vidisha. Please, stop, I have some questions for you."

"I can't. We can't... I mean, we have things we have to do. The play..." Prisi's heart was pounding.

"Let's go, girls," she said to her friends. "We've got to get out of here."

They finally made it to the front door of the school. MaiTae's uncle was standing there guarding the door. Luther Marshall was Highland Park's chief of police, and the girls were very glad to see him.

"Oh, I'm so glad you're here, Uncle Luther," said MaiTae. "What's going on anyway?"

Chief Marshall was a wonderful and loving uncle, but today he was all business. "What do you girls know about some missing ruby that is supposed to belong to the Queen of England?" he asked. He wasn't smiling. "There must be a dozen television stations here, and twice that many newspaper and radio reporters. Look over there. Those men are with the FBI."

Prisi gulped. "There goes my exclusive story for the *Slumber Girls Gazette*," she muttered.

"What did you say, Prisi?"

"Oh, nothing, Mr. Marshall. Nothing at all, really." She couldn't think. How did the news about the ruby leak out? Her father had agreed to put the ruby in the vault at the First National Bank, and both he and her mother had promised not to say a word to anyone. Her parents had spoken to the other girls' parents, too, and everyone knew how important it was to keep this a secret.

"Mr. Marshall, we've got to go inside and get ready for the play. Everyone will know soon what's going on, honest. We didn't do anything wrong, I promise. You can ask my dad." She looked up at him with her big green eyes.

"Oh, all right. Get inside. But if there's any trouble out here, I'm going to come looking for you." He hitched up his belt and looked around at the crowd that was gathering. He gave MaiTae a hug and winked at her. "You're sure you girls didn't do anything wrong?"

"Uncle Luther, you know we'd never do anything wrong, right?"

Before he could answer, the girls slipped past him and went into the school. Each lost in her own thoughts, the girls made their way to the auditorium.

"You guys didn't say anything to anyone, did you?" asked Prisi.

All three girls were staring at Prisi. Did she doubt their promise to each other?

"I know, I know. I'm sorry. It's just..." Prisi's voice trailed off for a moment. Then she said, "Rebecca Rodgers."

"Rebecca Rodgers?" asked Maya. "How would she know about the ruby?"

"Her brother works part-time at the bank. He must have seen my parents and told her, and she is desperate at this point to stop the play or at least make us look silly. "

"You're probably right," said MaiTae. "But the play still starts in less than two hours. We have to focus!"

"This is big," said Prisi.

"This is bigger than big," added Maya.

"Excuse me, girls." A large man had walked up the stairs to the stage and stood in front of them. "Which one of you is Priscilla Ballantine?"

"I am," squeaked Prisi. "Who are you?"

Another man joined the first one on the stage. "We're federal agents from Washington, D.C. The Queen of England contacted our agency to make certain nothing happens to the Missing Ruby of Vidisha. My partner here will escort your parents to the bank to retrieve it, and he will deliver it to you here. I will remain here and guard that other item the Queen promised you. I believe you know what I'm talking about. I will have it here for you at the proper time during the play."

"Huger than huge," whispered Skye.

"You girls go about your business. I'll be here just offstage, if you need anything," the agent reminded them.

The girls were filled to the brim with nervous energy as they made the last-minute preparations for The Mystical Dollhouse. It was all they could do to keep their minds on their work. This was going to be an evening that would never be forgotten in Highland Park.

They had expected to sell a handful of tickets to family and friends and maybe a few teachers. What Prisi saw when she peeked out at the audience from behind the curtain took her breath away.

"How many seats are there in the auditorium?" she asked, turning towards Skye.

"I don't know. Five hundred maybe. Why?"

"Look," said Prisi, pulling the curtain back a few inches so all the girls could see.

"There's not an empty seat anywhere," said Maya, her eyes wide with amazement.

"Huger than huger than huge," moaned Skye.

It was true. Word about the Missing Ruby of Vidisha and all of the television news trucks had spread like wildfire through the small town. Everyone, it seemed, wanted to be part of whatever was going to happen.

"I just wanted to write a play about my great-great-great-grandmother," said Prisi. "I didn't mean to...Oh my!"

Soon, it was time to begin. The lights in the auditorium dimmed, and the people in the audience grew quiet. A single spotlight illuminated a stool on the left side of the stage. Prisi came from behind the curtain and sat down. In her lap were the bundles of letters, each tied together by a faded red satin ribbon. In her right hand, she held a microphone.

"Sometimes, the most magical things can happen when you're playing," she began. "That's what we were doing, my friends and I. We were playing, exploring, just having fun."

Then she told the audience about discovering the key and how it had led them to the letters in the attic.

"These," she said, holding up the letters, "contain the story of the most extraordinary friendship between my great-great-great-grandmother Mary Ballantine and a princess. Tonight, you will learn, as we did, about how Mary Cambridge Ballantine befriended Princess Mary of Teck, and how their friendship blossomed over the years, although they were never to see one another again."

Prisi got down from the stool and walked to the center of the stage.

"This is a story that began in Florence, Italy, in the summer of 1884. It is about a princess who became Queen Mary of England and an American girl who became my great-great-great-grandmother. It is about a unique relationship. It is also, in a way, a mystery—one that was not solved until very recently. This is the story of a magical friendship and a mystical dollhouse."

She disappeared behind the curtain which opened a moment later to reveal an art gallery. Skye, as Princess Mary of Teck, and Maya, as Mary Cambridge, stood back to back looking at the paintings hanging on the wall. Sound asleep on a bench were two men, played by two of their classmates, who were hired by Princess Mary's father to protect her.

As the story of the play began to unfold, people in the audience who had come to the show over curiosity regarding the TV trucks soon were under the mystery's spell. The theater was silent except for the voices of the actors.

For the next scene, MaiTae had constructed a set which divided the stage in half. The whole theater was in darkness, until a spotlight illuminated the left half of the stage. There, Princess Mary could be seen sitting at a desk and writing a letter to Mary Cambridge. The princess began reading aloud from her first letter to her new friend. "10 August 1884—Dearest Mary, I cannot thank you enough for introducing yourself to me at the Palatine Gallery in the Pitti Palace a few weeks ago. I'm only sorry that we didn't have more time to get to know one another before those horrid men hurried me off like that. They work for my father who's hired them to escort me wherever I go."

She read a few more pages, and then the spotlight faded to darkness as another light came on to reveal the right half of the stage.

Mary Cambridge sat on her bed and continued reading aloud the letter from her new friend. At the end, she read: "Do remember, my new friend, to draw the flower in the lower left-hand corner of the envelope, as I have done. I do hate to sound so mysterious. It's just that so much of my life is controlled by others. I will instruct everyone that they are not to open any envelope bearing the picture of that flower, but rather they are to deliver it to me personally and without delay."

With those words, the first act ended. The theatre buzzed with excitement as the people looked at the flower drawn on the lower left-hand corner of their programs.

The second act began with one of the songs written for the play by Skye and Maya. It soon had everyone laughing as it told how the girls had fooled the princess's guards that day in the art gallery. The lyrics described the girls pretending to yawn in front of the already tired men, lulling them into falling asleep so the girls could talk.

Then more of the story of this remarkable relationship between the two young women was revealed. By the end of the second act, the audience had learned of the dollhouse and of the Queen's gift of the second bed.

"The dollhouse bed is yours," said Skye, now playing the part of Queen Mary, "as a symbol of our friendship that began so many years ago when we were much, much younger. Let it represent our childhoods and lives that we have shared over the years."

When the lights came up for the third act, the audience saw what appeared to be an attic filled with all kinds of antiques. The Slumber Girls, playing themselves, were seated in a circle reading the letters.

"Please write me when you receive it," read Prisi, "and tell me what you think of it. I can only imagine that you'll say, 'Who could sleep in such a thing?' Oh, we do get used to the finer things in life, don't we, dear friend?"

Prisi reached for the box, removed the lid with the carved crown on top, took out the dollhouse bed, and placed it on a table in the middle of the stage. The girls slowly backed away as all the lights dimmed and a single shaft of light surrounded the bed.

In the next scene, the girls were still in the attic. They began reading from the letter from Queen Elizabeth in which she told of the legendary Missing Ruby of Vidisha and the story of King Arthur's Cup. The audience was left speechless when Prisi removed the bedding from the Queen's dollhouse bed and tipped it over. When a most magnificent ruby dropped onto her palm, everyone in the theatre gasped.

The rumor that had spread through Highland Park that day was true. The Missing Ruby of Vidisha was indeed very real, and now it was very much resting in Prisi's hand.

A roar of applause filled the theatre as the curtains dropped and the lights came up. Understandably, the audience believed that to have been the final act of the play. As the people began to stand up and gather their coats, the lights flickered and then dimmed. The curtain began to rise slowly. The play was not yet over.

The people squinted as they tried to see what was on the stage. They soon saw what appeared to be a library. There were shelves of books and two swords hanging beneath a shield on the wall over a fireplace. In the corner of the room was a suit of armor.

A little girl, played by MaiTae's six-year-old sister Nisha, walked across the stage and climbed up on a chair. She reached for something on one of the shelves and then got down and turned around to face the audience. Without saying a word, she placed a large goblet on a small table. She reached into her pocket and pulled out the Missing Ruby of Vidisha and stuck it in the side of the goblet.

"King Arthur's Cup is complete once more," she said as the curtain began to close again. "And the Missing Ruby of Vidisha is no longer missing."

The people in the theatre were on their feet clapping and whistling and shouting. No one was louder or more enthusiastic than Vice Principal Vargas.

In interview after interview after the play, Prisi explained the whole story of the letters, how she wrote to the Queen and what the Queen said in her letter to Prisi about the Missing Ruby of Vidisha, King Arthur's Cup—everything.

The Queen, said Prisi, had written that though the gift of the bed was intended for Prisi's great-great-great-grandmother, the Ruby of Vidisha, which had taken on mythical proportions in English lore, was by rights the property of the English people. If Prisi promised to return the gem, the Queen said she would offer something wonderful in return: the loan of the actual King Arthur's Cup for Prisi to use in the play.

It was a grateful and tired quartet of friends who gladly handed the goblet and the ruby to the waiting FBI agents. The night was a success. They had solved a decades-old mystery. Now it was time to go home, head to bed, and dream.

Chapter Fourteen
Queen for a Day

As a result of the play and the widespread television and newspaper publicity it brought the town of Highland Park, a special ceremony was held at City Hall. After a long and rather boring speech, Mayor Winston Wakefield presented Prisi and the other Slumber Girls a giant key to the city of Highland Park. It was a special key designed to look just like the smaller, antique key that started the whole adventure.

Next, Dr. Stewart Livingston, the school principal, stepped to the podium. "In recognition of your great accomplishments, it gives me great pleasure," he announced, "to crown you, Prisi Ballantine, Highland Park Middle School's Queen for a Day."

She was soon surrounded by the other Slumber Girls and all their families. Rebecca Rodgers sulked at the edge of the crowd. "So what?" she sneered to her friends. "Who wants a dumb key?"

Prisi wished she could split the honor into four equal pieces, one fabulous piece for each of the Slumber Girls to enjoy. Life just didn't seem like it could get much better.

On a Saturday morning a few weeks later, the Slumber Girls were sound asleep after one of their famous slumber parties at Prisi's house.

"Prisi, wake up." Prisi's mother was insistent. "All of you, get up and come downstairs for breakfast. I've something to show you."

Four rather groggy girls shuffled down the stairs and into the kitchen.

"What is it, Mom?" asked Prisi with a big yawn.

"It's right in front of you," her mother replied.

There on the kitchen table was a rather large envelope postmarked from Buckingham Palace and addressed to Mistress Priscilla Ballantine. There was a small flower drawn in the lower left-hand corner. Prisi was instantly awake. She opened it hurriedly and began reading.

"Oh...my...stars!" exclaimed Prisi.

"Come on, Prisi, share it. What is it? What what what!?" the others pleaded.

"You are not going to believe it," said Prisi.

"Read it, Prisi," said Skye. "Read it to us!"

It was a letter from the Queen of England. In it, the Queen extended to them a formal invitation for them to have tea with her at Buckingham Palace. "And you must promise to bring your fanciest hats," wrote the Queen. "I hope this will be a most enjoyable and educational trip. Also, please tell your friend MaiTae to bring the paper she wrote about my country. I would so love to read it."

"There's something else in here," said Prisi. She turned the envelope upside down and onto the table fell a thick packet of tickets for passage across the Atlantic Ocean to England aboard the luxurious ocean liner, the Queen Mary II. There were tickets for Prisi, Maya, MaiTae, Skye, and for everyone in their families.

"This is absolutely mind-boggling," said Prisi's mother as she slumped into a chair. "I simply can't believe it."

"MaiTae, I sure hope you got a good grade on that paper," said Prisi with a laugh.

About this Story
What is fact and what is not?

The Mystical Dollhouse is what is called "historical fiction," which means it is part fiction and part non-fiction. In historical fiction, the writer makes up a story based on real events and sometimes real people.

In this story, the dollhouse of Queen Mary is quite real. It was built for the reasons that are mentioned in the book. The purpose of Queen Mary's Dolls' House was to showcase the works of England's craftsmen and artisans. The hope was that people from all over the world would see their talent and would hire them and buy their products. As you've learned, it is a most unusual dollhouse. There was only one bed constructed for the Queen's bedroom in the dollhouse. The second bed referred to in this story is fiction and is used to demonstrate the friendship between these two women.

Princess Mary of Teck (Queen Mary), of course, was a real person. Mary Cambridge Ballantine, however, is a fictional character, as are the Slumber Girls and their friends (though you probably know people who may be like them).

The letters between Queen Mary and Mary Cambridge Ballantine are also fiction, but they are a great way to convey the story of *The Mystical Dollhouse.*

The Missing Ruby of Vidisha and King Arthur's Cup? They, too, are fictional. But the Black Prince's Ruby which the story says adorns the imperial state crown of England? The Black Prince's Ruby and the imperial state crown are quite real. The crown, worn by the King or Queen of England on special occasions, contains nearly three thousand precious pearls and diamonds and other gems.

A Brief Biography of Queen Mary
(1867-1953)

Princess Mary of Teck

The Picture above is of King George V and Queen Mary. On the right, King George V is seen wearing the imperial state crown (the dark gem in the middle is the Black Prince's Ruby).

The story of Princess Mary of Teck, as told in *The Mystical Dollhouse*, is true. Financial difficulties did force her family to leave England in 1883. They traveled throughout Europe and stayed for a while in a villa in Florence, Italy. The princess loved art galleries. So while we don't know if she ever visited the Palatine Gallery mentioned in this story, it is certainly possible.

Princess Mary and her family returned to England in 1885 and lived for a time in White Lodge in Richmond Park, a short distance from downtown London. In 1893, she married Prince George of Windsor, at which time she became Her Royal Highness the Duchess of York. They had six sons and a daughter.

In 1910, her husband's father, King Edward VII, died. She became Queen Mary and her husband became King George V. When her husband died in 1936, their son Prince Edward ascended to the throne as King Edward VIII. He later gave up his role as king and was replaced by his brother who became King George VI. When he died, Queen Mary's granddaughter, Princess Elizabeth, became Queen of England, and she is still the Queen today.

Queen Mary was a tall woman with honey-colored hair and blue eyes. She didn't let much of her personality show through to the public and so most thought her to be either shy or overly stiff and serious. Apparently, as she pointed out in one of her letters to Prisi's great-great-great grandmother, she was quite a different person at home.

Queen Mary was a close and important advisor to her husband, and together they helped guide England through both World War I and World War II, working tirelessly to support British troops.

Queen Mary died in 1953 at the age of 85.

Queen Mary's Dolls' House

The Royal Collection © 2005 Her Majesty Queen Elizabeth II Photographer: David Cripps

The Entrance Hall

The Royal Collection © 2005 Her Majesty Queen Elizabeth II Photographer: David Cripps

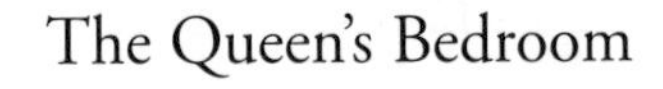

The Queen's Bedroom

The Royal Collection © 2005 Her Majesty Queen Elizabeth II

The Dining Room

The Royal Collection © 2005 Her Majesty Queen Elizabeth II

The Library

Although a few, very special children have played with it, Queen Mary's Dolls' House is definitely not a toy. It was, as the story of *The Mystical Dollhouse* points out, designed to help advertise to the world the enormous and varied talents of England's people.

Designed by the renowned architect Sir Edward Lutyens, it first began as a suggestion by the Princess Mary Louise, a cousin of King George V. The dollhouse was so intricate and exacting in detail that it accurately reflects the finest royal houses of England of its time.

Sir Lutyens wrote: "Let us devise and design for all time something which will enable future generations to see how a king and queen of England lived in the twentieth century, and what authors, artists, and craftsmen of note there were during their reign."

The dollhouse required the work of approximately fifteen hundred people over a three-year period. When finished, it contained more than forty rooms on four floors and was truly a palace in miniature. There are two working elevators and electric lights and chandeliers that operate from tiny switches on the walls. There are five bathrooms complete with hot and cold running water and toilets that flush.

Each room is elaborately furnished. There are original paintings created by the most famous artists of their time. Perhaps the most remarkable room is the library where there are leather-bound volumes written (many in their own hand) by the favorite authors of the era. Among them are tiny books by Sir Arthur Conan Doyle, Rudyard Kipling, Thomas Hardy, and many others.

The linens, the china, and the silver serving pieces were all recreated in miniature by the manufacturers of the life-size pieces that were in use at Windsor Castle. There is a miniature grand piano that actually works and a gramophone (a record player) that can play tiny records. The children's nursery contains little toys and furniture and a working stage for Peter Pan plays. In the princess's bedroom, Sir Lutyens really did place a tiny pea beneath the mattress, just as in the fairytale, "The Princess and the Pea."

The Queen's bedroom, with its walls covered in silk fabric, contains the canopy bed referred to in this story. The bedcover is made of blue silk and quilted with hundreds of the tiniest of pearls.

The royal gardens outside the house are beautifully "planted" with flowers, hedges, and stately trees—all made of rubber and metal. The miniature lawn mowers actually work.

The attention to detail throughout every room of the dollhouse is truly mind-boggling.

More than a half-million people visit Queen Mary's Dolls' House in Windsor Castle each year. The money collected for admission is used to fund the charities of the Queen of England.

Selected Bibliography

In addition to extensive Internet research and numerous encyclopedias, these are some of the main sources upon which I relied in the writing of *The Mystical Dollhouse.*

Matriarch—Queen Mary and the House of Windsor
Anne Edwards

William Morrow and Company, Inc.,
New York City, New York, 1984

Queen Mary's Dolls' House—Official Guidebook
Royal Collection Enterprises, Ltd., St. James's Palace,
London, England, 2004

Queen Mary's Dolls' House
Mary Stewart-Wilson, photographs by David Cripps
The Bodley Head, Ltd., London, England, 1988

"Queen Mary's Dolls' House"
British Broadcasting Company video, London, England, 1989

"Royal House for Dolls"
David Jeffery, photographs by James L. Stanfield
National Geographic, Washington, D.C., November 1980